THE
Nº1 CAR
SPOTTER

More books by Atinuke:

Anna Hibiscus

Hooray for Anna Hibiscus!

Good Luck, Anna Hibiscus!

Have Fun, Anna Hibiscus!

Anna Hibiscus' Song

THE N°1 CAR SPOTTER

by Atinuke

illustrated by Warwick Johnson Cadwell

Kane Miller
A DIVISION OF EDC PUBLISHING

First American Edition 2011
Kane Miller, A Division of EDC Publishing

First published in Great Britain 2010 by Walker Books Ltd
87 Vauxhall Walk, London SE11 5HJ

For information contact:
Kane Miller, A Division of EDC Publishing
P.O. Box 470663
Tulsa, OK 74147-0663
www.kanemiller.com
www.edcpub.com

Library of Congress Control Number: 2010943435

Printed and bound in the United States of America
1 2 3 4 5 6 7 8 9 10
ISBN: 978-1-61067-051-7

For my brother Ben
Writer, Adventurer and Car Spotter
A.

To my gang, D, S, H and W
W.J.C.

The No.1 Car Spotter

On the continent of Africa, you will find
my country. In my country there are many
cities, all with skyscrapers, hotels, offices.
There are also many smaller towns, all with
tap water and electricity and television.
Then there is my village, where we only talk
about such things.

Our village has a few compounds and many goats and several cows. It is in between the forest and the river and the road. The main road. The road brings cars past our village; many cars speeding towards the cities and the towns.

There are some few people in our village.

My best friend, Coca-Cola, lives in one compound with his old grandmother, his newborn sisters, Sunshine and Smile, and his mother, Mama Coca-Cola.

My sister's best friend, Nike, lives in another compound with her two elder brothers, Emergency and Tuesday, and her father, Uncle Go-Easy.

Beke, Bisi and Bola, the small children, live with their mother, Mama B, and Auntie Fine-Fine.

There are other people, in other compounds, but these are the people who know me well.

I live in a compound with my grandfather (who taught me everything I know), with my grandmother (who wants me to obey everything *she* knows), with my sister, Sissy, (who thinks I know nothing) and with my mother, who loves and feeds and looks after us all. My father, of course, lives in the city.

Let me introduce myself. My name is Oluwalase Babatunde Benson. But everybody calls me No. 1. The No. 1.

I am the No. 1 car spotter in my village. Car spotting is the only hobby in this village. Grandmother, Mama and all the aunties think that no such hobby should be allowed.

"Spotting cars does not take the goats to grass," Grandmother complains.

"It does not water the cows," Mama insists.

"Cars do not collect firewood," Auntie Fine-Fine confuses.

"Or carry yams from the fields," Mama Coca-Cola agrees.

"Cars won't fill your belly," Sissy joins in.

Sissy thinks spotting cars should be banned by the government. Sissy thinks that because I spot cars I am not doing my share of the work. It is not true. I work hard all day. I do everything Mama and Grandmother and Coca-Cola's mother and my Auntie Fine-Fine and Uncle Go-Easy and everybody else in the village tell me to do. But while I am doing it I spot cars!

Who can help spotting cars when the road runs directly past the village? It is what we men do.

Grandfather, sitting under the iroko tree in the center of the village, shouts, "Firebird!"

Uncle Go-Easy, waist-deep in the river, pulling in his nets, shouts, "Peugeot 505!"

Tuesday and Emergency, clearing the bush for a new field, hear an engine and shout, "Mercedes 914!"

Coca-Cola and I, high in the palm trees collecting nuts, shout, "Aston Martin DB5!"

Our village might be a poor village, lost in the bush, but a No. 1 road goes directly past it.

And I am the No. 1 car spotter! I can spot them before I see them. From the sound of their engines, running sweet or backfiring, I know them.

"Daewoo! Suzuki! Land Cruiser!"

It was Grandfather who taught me to be a car spotter. He spends his old age under the iroko tree watching the road. When I was a baby I stayed with him there in the shade of the tree while Mama worked on our farm. Grandfather taught me my ABC. My 123.

"Peugeot, Passat, Porsche …!"

What Grandfather does not know about spotting cars is not to know.

Grandfather and I love all cars. But I love the Corolla the best. It is the No. 1-and-only car of our village!

One time when I was very small I heard its engine from far. Grandfather told me what it was.

"Toyota Corolla," he said.

He held me up on my small legs to see. I saw dust. I saw smoke. I saw the Toyota Corolla crawl into the village. I saw it cut out right in front of me. I saw the driver call a taxi to return to the city with his head in his hands.

Since then the Corolla has been there in the heart of the village. Every time my cousin Wale the mechanic comes from the town he looks at it and shakes his head. It will not go. It will never carry us around like rich people. But it is still my favorite car. Often I dream I am driving this car along the road, fast!

"No. 1, what are you dreaming about! Go and carry the yams from the field!" shouted Mama suddenly.

"Pick mango and orange! Ripe and sweet!" 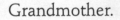 called Grandmother.

"Bring my beans!" commanded Mama Coca-Cola.

"The palm oil! The palm oil!" Auntie Fine-Fine joined in.

I started to run in all directions at once. Coca-Cola and Sissy and Emergency and Tuesday and Nike joined me.

Even Beke, Bisi and Bola started carrying baskets higher than themselves from the storeroom! All of our mothers and aunties and grandmothers were shouting at once.

The next day was market day. We would sell our palm oil and our yams, our onions, our tomatoes and our chili peppers, our baskets and our dried fish, our oranges, mangos, rice ...

With the money we would buy the important things we needed that only money can buy. Salt, sugar, kerosene for lamps, pencils and shoes for school. Sweets. Those things we cannot grow in our fields. Or pick from the trees of the forest. Or hunt in the bush. Or fish from the river.

I was running back with a basket of ripe mangos on my head when I heard a sharp crack.

Grandmother screamed and all the aunties started crying. Emergency and Tuesday had been pulling the old wooden cart into position, ready to load with all our goods for market.

"We heard a crack!" wailed Mama B.

"Like a gun firing," moaned Mama Coca-Cola.

"But it was the cart don' die-o!" Mama cried.

"Only God can save us now!" wept Auntie Fine-Fine.

They were gathered around the cart, wringing their hands and tearing at their clothes. Coca-Cola and Sissy and Nike and I pushed in to see.

The cart had broken! Snapped in half!

"How will I sell my palm oil?" wailed
Auntie Fine-Fine.

"How will I sell my yams?" wailed Mama.

"How will I sell my oranges and mangos?"
wailed Grandmother.

"No pencils for school," Sissy sobbed.

"No sweets." Coca-Cola and I looked at
each other.

"This cart must be fixed!" shouted Mama B.

Coca-Cola and I ran to help Grandfather up from under the iroko tree. Grandfather used to be a carpenter. The village carpenter. He walked stiffly around the cart. Then he shook his head.

"This one will never go again!" he said.

"You see!" shouted Grandmother. "This is where car spotting has got you! You are now a useless old man."

Grandfather shook his stick at her. "In the days when this village was full of men we would have cut a tree, planed the wood and fixed the cart. It is the village that has become useless. Not the man!" he shouted.

Grandmother sighed. She knew it was true. All of the men of the village (except for Grandfather and Uncle Go-Easy) now lived in the city, trying to find jobs and earn money to pay for shoes and medicine and schooling for us, their families. My father was there. Coca-Cola's father was there. Even some of the women were there.

"Before-before our village was so full of women," Mama sighed, "we could have carried everything to market on our heads."

"Now everybody loves to live in the city," wailed Mama Coca-Cola.

"And we are left with a broken old cart!" said Grandmother, sucking her teeth. "And a broken old man."

"And how will we get to market and back?" cried Sissy.

Grandfather sadly shook his head. He sat down on the back of the Corolla to rest his old-old legs.

I looked at the broken cart. I looked at Grandfather sitting on the broken Corolla.

"Can't you make that machine work?" demanded Grandmother unreasonably, pointing to the Corolla. "You who love cars so much?"

Grandfather shook his head once again. "This one," he said, patting the Corolla, "will never go again."

"Is that all you can say!" shouted the women.

Grandfather shrugged his shoulders and raised his hands.

I looked from Grandfather on the Corolla to the women by the cart. Suddenly a light switched on inside my brain. I, who did not even know I had electricity! The electricity fired my legs. I started to run.

"No. 1! Where are you going?" shouted Mama.

"Oluwalase Babatunde Benson! Stop!" shouted Grandmother. "Come here!"

"Wait for me!" shouted Coca-Cola.

I did not stop. I could not wait. The current was running and there was no OFF switch. I did not stop at the river. I did not stop at the farm. I ran all the way through the bush to the town and it took me from morning until night was about to fall.

I zigzagged through the houses until I saw my cousin's corrugated iron shop. The ground all around was littered with rags and scraps of metal and black with the oil that cars like to drink.

"Wale! Wale! Wale!" I banged on the door.

"Come back tomorrow!" his voice replied.

"Is me! No. 1!" I shouted.

The door opened.

"Ah-ah! Oluwalase Babatunde Benson!"

 my cousin exclaimed. "Small brother!" He acknowledged that indeed we had the same grandmother and the same grandfather. "Way-tin?" He wanted to know what I was doing here in town all alone, banging on his door in the night.

I told him my idea. I told him everything.
"Slow down, slow down," he said at first.
And then he said, *"Na-wa-oh!"* which means
"Wow!"

He called his friends and drew my idea in
the dirt for them to look at. I was just a small
boy compared to them. But I had a big idea.
They nodded their heads, collected their
equipment and together we
ran back to the village.

When we arrived it was deep night. Grandmother and Mama were waiting for me, crying.

"Do you want to kill me!" Mama shouted.

"Do you not know that crocodiles and leopards and towns can eat a small boy like you!" Grandmother shouted.

"Lazy boy!" shouted Sissy from the house. She had to do my work that day.

But I did not stop to defend myself. I kept running until we reached the Corolla. We offloaded the equipment and set to work right away. There was no time for palava. No time for wahala. No time for all this shouting. Tomorrow was market day!

The whole village woke when metal started grinding against metal. All the people gathered around the red sparks flying from the screaming Corolla. Only Coca-Cola's old grandmother stayed sleeping on her mat.

Grandfather came to stand beside me. He put his hand on my shoulder.

"*Ku ise, o, eyin omo mi*. Good work," he said to Wale and his friends.

"*A dupe, o,* Grandfather," they replied. "Thank you."

When the stars began to fade, metal kissed red metal together. Dawn was bright in the sky. The machines were silent. The mechanics were still.

Grandmother opened her mouth.

"Shh!" said Grandfather.

I left the chopped-up Corolla and went down to the river. I brought all the cows to the village and hitched them all up to ...

"Na-wa-oh!" gasped my mother.

"Na-wa-oh!" shouted my grandmother.

"Na-wa-oh!" whispered my sister.

"Sorry-o!" they all said, again and again. "Sorry."

Mama Coca-Cola and Auntie Fine-Fine were screaming with joy.

Uncle Go-Easy was walking around and around our new cart, shaking his head with wonder.

I led the cows around the village. It worked perfectly.

Wale and his friends whooped and shouted and jumped into one another's arms. They had won the World Cup for car cutting.

Grandfather shook their hands. Then he shook my hand. "Congratulations," he said.

"The fruit does not fall far from the tree," said Mama.

Grandfather and I smiled at each other. It was inside my head that the light switch had come on. But it was Grandfather who had done the wiring.

Then Grandfather shouted, "Where are the yams and the onions and the peppers and the mangos and the oranges and the dried fish and the rice and the palm oil? Is this village not going to market today?"

I laughed to see Mama and the aunties and the grandmothers all jump up and start to run around in every direction.

The No. 1 car spotter. That's me! Getting our village to market and back … in our new No. 1 Toyota Cow-rolla!

No.1 Goes to Market

Come on, you remember me! Oluwalase
Babatunde? I am the No. 1 car spotter.
The No. 1 car spotter in my village.
Maybe the No. 1 car spotter in the world.

   Look at us now, the No. 1 village,
escorting our new Toyota Cow-rolla into
market!

We had loaded it with baskets piled high with yams, onions, tomatoes, plantains, chili peppers, mangos, oranges, dried fish, rice, palm oil.

"This cart strong-o!" crowed Mama.

"This one no fit break-o!" agreed Grandmother.

"This cart fit carry rock and stone!" said Mama B proudly.

We sang praise songs to the cart all the way to market and when the market people saw us arrive with our No. 1 vehicle you should have heard them shout!

"Wha' is dis? Can you believe it?"

"Ah-ah! Check out village pick-up!"

"Na new off-road style!"

Every man, woman and child ran to see how our ordinary village cows could be pulling one wonda-full imported Corolla.

Mama and the aunties got busy offloading our goods, but us men got busy telling everybody wha' happen.

"My boy, he achieve electricity for brain!" Grandfather boasted.

"The mechanic boys were sparking all night!" Uncle Go-Easy joined in from his dried fish stall.

"Sha! It was easy!" Wale crowed.

And then all the women stopped listening to us because Mama and the aunties had finished offloading and suddenly we were surrounded by fat red tomatoes, skinny, biting chili peppers, rice fresh on stalk, pungent dried fish, golden palm oil. The best in the market!

The women were remembering what they had come to market for. Then Mama Coca-Cola started frying akara … and then all the men were gone!

Grandfather went to sleep in the cart. Wale disappeared with his friends. But I was kept busy helping Mama and the aunties and Uncle Go-Easy to sell.

"Bag – you need bag?"
Mama questioned a customer.
"Bring bag for this lady! Bring
bag for this lady!"

"Change!"
bellowed Mama
Coca-Cola. "I
need small change!"

"Fresh water!"
coughed Mama B.

"Thief!"
screamed
Grandmother. "Catch
that boy! Reclaim my
mango!"

I was busy running back and forth,
back and forth in the heat, but I did not
complain, not for one second. Nor did Sissy
and Nike and Coca-Cola and Emergency
and Tuesday. The more tomatoes and fish
and oil we sold, the more pencils and sugar
and flip-flops our mothers would buy for
us. So we were like Olympic runners, quick
off the mark. And if we jumped the
gun, nobody complained.

When the sun was high in the sky the customers started to dry up. The baskets were low. The best of everything had gone. Mama and the aunties did not need our help anymore.

But I saw Auntie Fine-Fine beckon to Sissy. She whispered into Sissy's ear and Sissy started to smile. Sissy's smile grew so wide I wanted to know what she thought she would put there.

I could read Auntie Fine-Fine's lips. "How much? Ask how much."

When Sissy ran off into the market I beckoned to Coca-Cola. We followed Sissy past the plantain sellers and the plastic cup traders, past the goats and the chickens and the plastic shoe traders and the mountains of yard cloth.

Suddenly Sissy stopped by a little stall loaded with small-small bottles and jars. The containers were all different colors of red and pink and so on. Some shaped long like tube, some small-small bottles with lid like fat pencil, some round flat boxes, all with painted women smiling wide.

I braked behind a mountain of wax cloth. Coca-Cola crashed into me and we narrowly avoided toppling the new cloth into the dirt. I gave Coca-Cola a dirty look.

"No brake light! No indicator!" he hissed at me. "I go book you!"

"Sorry, officer, sorry. I beg you!" I tried not to laugh.

Sissy turned around and looked. She shouted, "Don' think I don' see you there, No. 1! Did anybody send you here? I don't think so. Jus' wait till I tell Mama!"

Everybody at the stalls heard Sissy's words. They all turned around to look. My face became hot. I turned and ran back. Coca-Cola got there before me. Hiding behind the Cow-rolla.

Grandmother looked at me with narrowed eyes. Quickly I looked down at the ground. It was littered with squashed tomatoes and sweet wrappers. I grabbed Mama's broom and started to sweep. Grandmother smiled at me.

I was just about to load the empty baskets onto the cart and take the opportunity to court marshal Coca-Cola for deserting me under enemy fire when Sissy arrived back, empty-handed.

I busied myself sweeping. Sissy looked at me and opened her mouth loud. But before she could speak, Auntie Fine-Fine beckoned to her. "Price? Price?" I saw her ask.

Sissy bent and whispered in her ear, then straightened to look at me.

As she opened her mouth again Mama

B called, "Where have you been, Sissy? I want you and Nike to take Beke and Bisi and Bola to buy plastic shoe. Good quality and cheap. Go now while there is still time!"

Sissy's mouth was still open. She was looking at me. But Mama shut her mouth for her by saying, "Did you not hear your auntie? What are you waiting for? Go!"

Sissy and Nike went off into the market, holding onto Beke and Bisi and Bola.

I put down my brush and heaved a sigh of relief.

Auntie Fine-Fine was calling after Sissy, but Sissy was gone. And shopping with Beke and Bisi and Bola would take a LONG time. You did not need a brain to know that. Auntie Fine-Fine looked around despondent and caught me looking at her. She smiled.

"No. 1!" she called.

I tried to hide behind my broom.

"No. 1!" Auntie Fine-Fine called again.

I saw Mama look at me when I did not answer.

"Yes, Auntie," I answered.

"Come here, good boy!" Auntie Fine-Fine called. "I want you to do something for me."

Mama narrowed her eyes at me, waiting for me to answer. What can a boy my size do in such a situation?

"Yes, Auntie!" I said again and went to Auntie Fine-Fine.

"Do you know the stall that sells many small-small bottles and containers?" she asked.

"Yes, Auntie," I replied. I looked around desperately for Coca-Cola. His legs were disappearing into the Cow-rolla. They were going nowhere with me.

"I want you to go there and buy me …" Auntie Fine-Fine gestured for me to come closer.

Grandmother looked up.

"*Lipstick*," Auntie Fine-Fine whispered and pressed money in my hand.

Grandmother's eyes widened.

"Go!" Auntie Fine-Fine said.

I looked at Mama. She had not heard Auntie Fine-Fine say lipstick. Her eyes said obedience *or else*.

So I went. Past the plantains and plastic cups and the chickens and the goats and plastic shoes, where Sissy stared at me and sucked her teeth. When I got to the cloth stall again I stopped.

I prayed that the stall I was headed for had gone. I did not know what lipstick was. But it was women's business. And women's business was not for a small boy like me. I did not want the whole market to look at me again.

But there it was, with all its small-small bottles and jars and boxes the color of chili peppers and this time even more ... girls.

I was ready to wait behind the cloth until they were gone when a big man pushed me out into the open.

"Can' you let a man pass!" he shouted.

All the girls turned around. Suddenly I opened my shoulders and made myself stand tall. I was the No. 1. What was I afraid of?

I pushed my way to the front of the stall as if it was nothing to me to be there. I stared at the bottles and jars. Which one was *lipstick*?

The trader leaned over the jars and looked at me.

"Wha' is a small boy like you doing here?"
he said. "This is not where you will find
football match or computer game!"

The girls started to giggle. Quickly
I picked up one of the glass jars as if I
knew what I was doing. I pushed Auntie
Fine-Fine's money into the trader's hand.
Then I ran away.

I ran all the way back and gave the jar to Auntie Fine-Fine. I started to join Coca-Cola in the Cow-rolla.

But before I had the chance to walk two steps Auntie Fine-Fine cried out, "What is this *thing*? This is not what I asked you to buy! What am I supposed to do with this? WHERE IS MY MONEY?"

All the women turned to look at me. It was too late to run.

"No. 1!" shouted Mama. "What have you done?"

"Nothing, Mama," I answered. "I do not know."

"What kin' answer is that?" my mother demanded. I could see plenty of trouble coming and no sweets after all my hard work.

Mama stood up. Grandfather woke up
to see what all the commotion was about.
Coca-Cola's feet were trembling on my
behalf. Auntie Fine-Fine was still shouting.
Everybody was looking at me.

Suddenly Grandmother said, "Don' blame
the boy. This woman sent him to buy
lipstick!"

There was a sudden silence as
Grandmother's words were absorbed. Then
all the aunties started to laugh. Mama
laughed the loudest and patted
my shoulders.

Auntie Fine-Fine stopped shouting and started to cry. The laughing aunties gathered around to comfort her. Auntie Fine-Fine's mouth was open so wide there was no room in her face for her eyes.

"My money-o! This useless thing for all my money-o!" she kept crying.

Sissy arrived back just then, dragging Beke, Bisi and Bola. She looked at me. She looked at Auntie Fine-Fine. She looked at the jar in Auntie Fine-Fine's hand.

Sissy took the jar. She winked at me. She opened the jar, bent down and busied herself at Auntie Fine-Fine's feet. None of the aunties took any notice. They were all too busy comforting Auntie Fine-Fine. Suddenly Sissy stood up.

The aunties shrieked. Grandmother fell from her stool. Coca-Cola's head appeared over the top of the cart. Grandfather shouted, *"What?"* We all stared at Auntie Fine-Fine's feet.

Auntie Fine-Fine closed her mouth in order to see what was going on. She looked at our bulging eyes. She looked down to see what we were ogling. Her toenails! They were *pink*. Bright hibiscus *pink*.

Auntie Fine-Fine did not move for almost one minute. Then slowly she smiled. She laughed. She clapped her hands. She rose to her feet and started to admire herself. All the other aunties commenced laughing and clapping too.

Auntie Fine-Fine started to dance right there in the market!

Then Auntie Fine-Fine came towards me. Grandfather gripped my shoulder.

"*Cleva boy!*" Auntie Fine-Fine shouted.

"Go buy me one!" Mama B demanded.

"Red one! I want red one!" yelled Mama Coca-Cola.

"*Cleva boy!*" Auntie Fine-Fine repeated, squeezing my cheek.

She pressed some money in my hand.
It was enough to buy sweets *and* fritters!
I smiled my No. 1 smile.

Now all the aunties were pressing money
on me. "Go and buy! Go and buy!" they
shouted.

I looked up at Grandfather. His eyebrows
were raised. Mama was laughing. Grandmother
shaking her head. Trouble had been shaking
me with its teeth, now it was throwing me
back to that stall.

It was time to go. We were tired. We were happy to load our salt and sugar and kerosene and cloth into the Cow-rolla and ride home. Speaking for myself, my stomach was so full of fritters and sweets I could not have walked.

But not Auntie Fine-Fine. Auntie Fine-Fine insisted on walking. "I can see my feet better like this," she said.

I looked down at Auntie Fine-Fine's feet
flashing in the road.

"Porsche," I said. Coca-Cola looked up
and down the road.

"Where?" he asked.

I nodded down at Auntie Fine-Fine's toes
flashing in the dirt. Coca-Cola and I laughed.
Ten pink Porsche convertibles were stirring
up the dust!

7UP

Greetings from the No. 1. The No. 1 car spotter in my village, maybe the No. 1 car spotter in the whole world!

One time I came close to losing my name. Only one time. It happen like this. When I am not with Grandfather under the iroko trees spotting cars, I am with Coca-Cola. Coca-Cola is my tight friend. He has the coolest name in the village.

Coca-Cola got his own name because his mother, Mama Coca-Cola, sells akara by the roadside. She fries exactly the right blend of beans and onions and chili peppers and salt to hit a person's pocket. The smell travels straight from the person's nose direct to the person's belly, from there it goes direct to the person's cash, which lands immediately in Mama Coca-Cola's hand. And the akara tastes so good that once you have eaten one you have to eat more. And once you have eaten more you need to take something to make room for more. And nothing washes akara down better (Mama Coca-Cola knows) than cold soft drinks.

So Mama Coca-Cola stores her soft drinks in the river in order to serve them chilled. It is Coca-Cola's job to carry the Coca-Cola, Fanta, 7UP and Sprite from the river to the customer. And Mama Coca-Cola's shorthand way of telling him that customers are waiting for drinks is to shout, "Coca-Cola!" at the top of her voice.

Once upon a time Coca-Cola had a traditional name but now everybody just calls him Coca-Cola.

One day I was with Coca-Cola in his compound when it was time for him to eat. Of course Mama Coca-Cola called me to eat also. Akara is not the only food Mama Coca-Cola knows how to cook well. I ate and ate and ate; in the end my belly weighed so much I could not carry myself back to my own compound to sleep. When Coca-Cola lay down for the night I collapsed next to him.

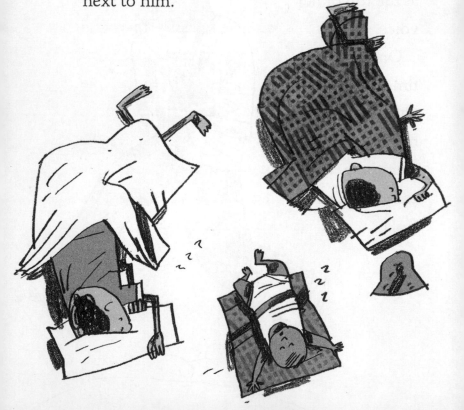

In the morning as soon as I woke up I knew that I was in Mama Coca-Cola's house. Instead of being surrounded by the noises of my family already at work, sweeping the compound and washing clothes, I was surrounded by snores.

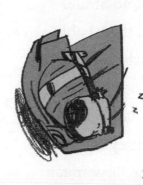

Coca-Cola's family loves to sleep. Maybe it is because of the mountain of food they consume on a nightly basis. A full belly loves to sleep, it has no need to complain, no need to wake.

The rest of the village wakes early. Before the first cock-crow, before the first light. And every morning, when we are already hard at work, we always hear Mama Coca-Cola wake with a shout. Then we see her run down to her stall, still tying her wrappa, to begin frying akara with Sunshine and Smile still at her breast and the first bus already past!

This morning they were still snoring when I awoke. It was dark, but I sat up immediately. Grandmother would be needing me to collect firewood. Mama would be calling me to hoe the fields. Sissy would need my help with the goats. My sitting up woke Sunshine and Smile. They opened their baby eyes, and started to laugh, then cry for food. Mama Coca-Cola opened her eyes. She looked to the window to see how much of the morning had already passed.

When she saw that the sun had not even reached the sky, that only the cockerels crowing and the sounds of the village awakening were indications of its impending arrival, Mama Coca-Cola was so happy.

She jumped to her feet, squeezed my cheeks, and started shouting, "Onions! Beans! Frying pan! Stool!"

Coca-Cola shot off his mat and started to run around. As I was an able-bodied boy in the vicinity of a shouting mama I started to run around as well.

By the time we had collected everything, Mama Coca-Cola had fed Sunshine and Smile and adjusted her wrappa. She was ready to go down to her position on the road. Before the village knew what was happening the smell of frying akara had filled the air and those who had not yet eaten found their bellies propelling their legs towards last night's leftovers.

The first bus arrived.

Coca-Cola and I started to run. We laughed as we ran to the river. Happily I loaded my arms with cold bottles. Running for Mama Coca-Cola meant akara. For breakfast, lunch and dinner.

I was licking my fingers when the second bus arrived.

"Coca-Cola! 7UP!" Mama Coca-Cola shouted.

I was happy to run back to the river. I would run anywhere for Mama Coca-Cola's akara.

On my way I passed Sissy, my sister, taking our goats to graze in the hot, dusty, dry bush.

"No. 1!" she shouted. "Come here and take the goats to grass!"

"I am answering Mama Coca-Cola!" I shouted back.

Sissy sucked her teeth. "Greedy boy!" she shouted.

I ignored her.

I was just licking my fingers when three BMWs stopped in front of Mama Coca-Cola's stall.

Coca-Cola and I started running. I passed Grandmother.

"No. 1! Firewood!" she shouted.

I shouted back again, "I answer Mama Coca-Cola!"

Grandmother shook her broom at me. "Just le' me catch you!" she shouted. But I knew she couldn't.

On the way back we passed the iroko tree. Emergency was sitting there with Grandfather.

"Mammy wagon!" Emergency shouted.

I looked at the road. There was the mammy wagon approaching, rocking from side to side with many, many passengers. I offloaded my bottles into Coca-Cola's arms and turned around to run back to the river for more.

"You are allowing your stomach to rule your legs!" Grandfather said on my way back.

I pretended I did not hear him.

The following morning I woke once again in Mama Coca-Cola's house. The previous evening I had allowed her to reward my hard work with another mountain of delicious food.

Once again I sat up in the dark. Sunshine and Smile started to clamor for food. Mama Coca-Cola opened her eyes and smiled.

By the time the first bus arrived, the akara was ready.

"Coca-Cola! 7UP!" Mama Coca-Cola shouted.

Fresh akara had fueled my engine. My legs were pistons carrying me down to the river.

On the way I passed Mama. She was
going to wash our clothes in the river.

"Good morning, Coca-Cola! Good
morning, 7UP!" she said.

My engine stuttered.

I passed Sissy and Nike, their
heads loaded with firewood.

"Look, it's the soft drinks!" said Sissy.

"Good morning, Coca-Cola!
Good morning, 7UP!" Nike
giggled.

My engine faltered.

On the way back from the
river we saw Uncle Go-
Easy. "You boys! Coca-Cola!
7UP!" he shouted. "Make
sure you no touch
my fishing net
when you go
for river!"

I braked immediately.

"Stop!" I shouted to Coca-Cola.

I loaded all my soft drinks on top of his.

"Wha' happen?" he asked.

"Tell your mother that Grandmother is waiting for me to sweep the yard, I have to escort our goats to the bush, and Sissy and Mama are waiting for me … to take care of … everything!"

"Don' you wan' eat akara?" Coca-Cola asked.

I did not answer. I ran into our compound.

"So!" Grandmother said. "Did your belly tire of superior food?"

"Yes! No, Grandmother," I replied looking meekly at the ground.

"What are you waiting for?" she snapped. "Sweep the compound! Take the cows to drink at the river! Take the goats to the bush! Don't come back until you have collected firewood! Go!"

Down by the river with the cows, I met Coca-Cola, his arms loaded with soft drinks. He looked sadly at me.

"Why don' you stay with me?" he asked.

"Coca-Cola," I said, "I am the No. 1. THE No. 1. I am not 7UP."

"But why?" said Coca-Cola. "W'a's wrong with 7UP?"

"Because," I said, "No. 1 is number ONE. Who wants to be called 7UP when he can be called NUMBER ONE? No. 1 is first in line. Seven has to wait until one, two, three, four, five and six have all passed before you reach him."

Coca-Cola said nothing. He looked at the river. Then he said, "I am Coca-Cola."

"That," I said, "is because Coca-Cola is the number one soft drink. Some people prefer Fanta. It is true. And some people prefer Sprite. Some people don't touch Coca-Cola. But Coca-Cola is still the number one."

And before either of us could say anything more we heard Mama Coca-Cola shouting, "Coca-Cola! Coca-Cola! Where is that boy?"

Coca-Cola ran back. I walked slowly back from the river with the cows. I passed the iroko tree. Grandfather was there. I stopped. Grandfather said nothing. He was watching the road. Suddenly my mouth opened.

"Coca-Cola is my tight friend," I said.

"I have noticed," said Grandfather.

"Now he is running back and forth, back and forth," I said as Coca-Cola ran past.

"Every two seconds," Grandfather said.

"I will help him." I said. "No. 7 is not so far behind No. 1."

"Your mother and grandmother and sister also need you –" Grandfather started to say.

"No. 1! No. 1!"

It was Auntie Fine-Fine.

"Your mother said I should call you," she said. "The palm nuts are ripe!"

Grandfather looked at me.

Quickly I returned the cows to the compound and turned towards the farm. Palm nuts give palm oil. Soup and stew are made with palm oil. Yam and plantain are fried in palm oil. Where there is nothing else we dip our soft food in palm oil. In fact, without palm oil, there is no such thing as good food.

As soon as I reached the farm, I attached my rope around my waist and started to climb.

I smiled. Who cannot be happy up in a tree? (At least in the first hour, before the back and legs begin to ache!)

From the ground
Mama and the
aunties were shouting,
"Make you hurry-o!"

"Let me not stand here all day waiting to collect!"

"Don' forget before you eat the oil, we have to press the nut!"

"Reach the top! Why go-slow?"

I pretend I cannot hear them. From high in the tree I can see the whole village, the whole road. There is Grandfather under the iroko tree. There is Grandmother supervising the children of the village and readying herself to press palm oil. And there is Coca-Cola and Mama Coca-Cola by the road, waiting for customers.

I look down the
dusty road again. In the
distance I can see dust. A lot of dust.
I lean out of my tree in the direction of
Mama Coca-Cola's stall.

"BUS!" I scream. "Bus come soon!"

Coca-Cola leaps up. He looks down the
road. He can see nothing. Mama Coca-Cola
shakes her head.

"BUS!" I scream again.

Again Coca-Cola leaps up. And this
time they recognize my voice. And they
remember that I am the No. 1. The No. 1 car
spotter in the village.

Mama Coca-Cola starts to cook akara
double time.

Coca-Cola runs fast to the river and carries
many bottles back to the stall. He has time
to make two journeys.

By this time the bus is announcing itself
with its growling engine.

From where I am
in the tree, I can see the bus stop
and passengers alight. I can see the bottles
of cold soft drinks dripping on the table. I
can see people digging in their wallets.

By the end of the day I have cut many
bunches of palm nuts, all of which Mama
and Grandmother are just now squeezing
into fresh, orange-red, tasty palm oil which
they will use to cook our food.

I have also alerted Mama Coca-Cola
to the imminent arrival of twenty-three
vehicles.

That night I am happy to be in my own compound with Mama and Grandmother and Grandfather and Sissy.

Outside the compound I can hear Mama Coca-Cola talking loudly to everybody.

"My stall is now the No. 1 stall. The No. 1 stall on the road. And it is because of that boy."

I catch Coca-Cola's eye peeping through the gateway. He smiles.

"That boy," I hear Mama Coca-Cola say to the whole village, "is truly the No. 1! The No. 1 car spotter on the road!"

No. 1 and the Wheelbarrow

It's me! The No. 1 car spotter! Spotting cars from the No. 1 spot under the iroko tree.

This is where Grandfather sits.

Grandfather, the No. 1 of all the No. 1s.

"It used to be that there was only one car on the road," Grandfather remembers. "The Peugeot –"

"403!" I shout. "Followed by 404."

"But now things are much more interesting," says Grandfather. "There are many more cars to spot, many more types to memorize, many more makes to identify.

"Take the Pontiac Firebird, for example," Grandfather sighs. "There is only one in the whole country. ONE. And it belongs to a university professor. This no be area-boy car. The Firebird! It used to pass by here any time Prof went to his village."

In the good old days Grandfather would challenge me. "Which one can you remember?"

"Aston Martin, Audi, Bentley, Cadillac, Citroën, Daewoo, Eclipse, Ferrari, Fiat, Ford, Golf, Honda, Isuzu, Jaguar, Jeep, Komatsu, Land Rover, Lamborghini, Lada, Mitsubishi, Nissan, Opel, Pontiac, Peugeot, Porsche, Rolls-Royce, Skoda, Saab, Toyota, Uno, Volvo, Vauxhall, VW, X-90, Yamaha, Zimmer ..."

And Grandfather would nod his head. "Good. Good."

Those were the good old days.

Then came the bad.

Grandfather and I were still under the iroko tree. But in silence, alone. Grandfather had sent away all the people who sometimes sat with him there. We watched the road. But we were not spotting cars. Our thoughts were in Grandmother's room.

Grandmother was sick. She could not come out of her room. It was clear to everybody, Grandmother needed medical doctor to perform miracle. Or she would die.

Grandfather counted all his money. Every naira note and kobo coin he had saved over the years. His money was not enough for medical miracle.

Mama counted all her money. All the money my father had sent her that she had managed to save. It was not enough for medicine.

Not even together with Grandfather's money. The money did not reach.

My father worked hard in the city to provide us all with shoes and school and medicine. Money like that can only be earned in the city.

My mother sent a message to my father for money. Money to save Grandmother's life.

Mama sent the message through one taxi driver who often passed our village on his way to and from the city. The taxi driver knew my father. He knew where my father worked as a gardener in a rich man's compound in the city.

But when the taxi driver next passed he told us that he had not found my father there. There was another man working as gardener in the rich man's compound and nobody knew what had happened to my father.

Since then Grandfather has not moved from the iroko tree. I have not moved from Grandfather. Grandmother cannot move from her bed. Mama does not move from Grandmother's room. And Sissy struggles alone with the goats and the cows and everything. She does not sing. She does not smile or laugh.

The aunties struggle on the farms with their babies on their backs and at their feet. Grandmother was no longer in the compound ready to look after them all. The aunties abandon their farms early in the day to bring us food.

"Eat! Eat!" they begged.

How could we eat? Grandmother was fading before our very eyes. And Papa had disappeared.

Suddenly Grandfather stood up. He looked down the road. I looked too. *What?* There was nothing.

Grandfather tried to walk towards the road. But in the time he had been sitting, sitting, sitting under the tree, his bones had become old and stiff. Grandfather fell down.

I shouted. Mama came from the house to see why. Sissy came to help me raise Grandfather from the ground.

When he was back on his feet Grandfather turned again towards the road, using my shoulder for a walking stick.

Then somebody came into view walking down the road. Grandfather forgot he was old. Grandfather tried to run.

Suddenly Grandfather was not alone in running. My legs and Sissy's legs were also possessed by joy. We overtook Grandfather.

"Papa! Papa! Papa!"

Mama came running out of Grandmother's room. "Akin! Akin! Akin!"

It was my father. Home! He took us all in his arms. He smelled of sweat and tiredness.

The whole village came to celebrate. They brought food for us again that night.

"You see," Auntie Fine-Fine whispered. "One problem has solved. The other will also solve."

"Now that he has returned, Old Mama will improve," agreed Uncle Go-Easy.

"He will look after everything," said Mama Coca-Cola. "You have no more need to worry."

On every face hope was shining. But not on Papa's face.

"Our son has returned!" I heard Grandfather whisper to Grandmother from the door of her room.

But when he thought everybody was asleep I head Papa say this: "My wife, I have no more job. Oga turned me out one month ago. Since then I have been applicant. I have been going from one place to another. They all say the same thing. No job. No job. No job. *Olori mi*, I have no money for doctor."

My father cried.

The next day I did not sit with Grandfather. I could see him under the iroko tree. He kept looking towards my mother's room. He was waiting for my father to come out and call a taxi to carry Grandmother to the medical center. He was wondering why his son did not come out quickly.

I stayed behind Mama Coca-Cola's stall. Mama Coca-Cola looked at me. She looked up at Grandfather. She looked for a long time at our quiet compound.

Mama Coca-Cola sighed. She cooked fresh akara for me.

"Four-by-four!" Coca-Cola shouted.

I looked up. Four-by-four was Mike.

The NGO. Non-Government Organization man. Call him what you like. He had come from the city to build the medical center. He had brought the palm nut press.

"Hi, Mike! Hi, Mike!" Coca-
Cola was shouting "Hi!" city-style
just like Mike had taught us. I did
not even feel like smiling.

Mike bought all of us cold drinks.
Me and Sissy and Coca-Cola and
Nike and Bisi and Bola and Beke and
Emergency and Tuesday and the others.

"How is Grandmother today?" Mike
looked at me.

I shook my head.

Mike looked sad. "She needs to go to
the medical center," he said. "I can give
her a lift there."

I shook my head. "No money for doctor,"
I said.

Mike looked sad. Then he smiled. "Hey,
I have something for you," he said.

I looked at him. Mike never gave us
money, but sometimes he had chocolate.
Sometimes he had chewing gum.

"Wheelbarrows!" said Mike. "Free to anybody who can sign. To improve village life."

Coca-Cola and I looked at each other.

"Come on," said Mike. "Surely smart kids like you can write your names?"

"I can do that!" I shouted.

Last time Cousin Overtime was here she had taught Sissy and Coca-Cola and me to write our names.

"Excellent!" said Mike. "This village could do with a few wheelbarrows!"

He took some papers from his four-by-four car and showed us where to sign.

"Wheelbarrows are to improve village life. Not for selling," he told us again.

Sissy, Coca-Cola and I nodded. "Yes, Mike. OK, Mike."

We signed. Then Mike unloaded three wheelbarrows from the back of his four-by-four.

Mama Coca-Cola was dancing and singing and clapping around Coca-Cola's wheelbarrow. It would carry many soft drinks back and forth from the river.

Mike smiled, beeped his horn and drove away.

Sissy and I slowly pushed our wheelbarrows up towards our compound. Papa was sitting under the iroko tree with Grandfather, at last. They both looked as stiff as the tree.

"What is this?" Papa asked.

"It is an NGO wheelbarrow, Papa," I replied.

"To improve village life," said Sissy.

Papa jumped to his feet and started to shout, "Who will pay for this?"

"They were free, Papa!" Sissy was crying.

I could see Papa was struggling to believe her.

"The NGO gave them to us, Papa," I said. "We only had to sign."

Papa looked at Grandfather.

"He is the man who brought us the palm oil press," Grandfather said. "The same one who built the school and the medical center. He is a good man."

For a long time Papa was silent. Then he said, "Will he come to take them back?"

"No, Papa," I said.

"And he does not expect us to pay later?" Papa asked.

"No, Papa," said Sissy, "they were free. To improve village life."

At last Papa nodded. He walked around the wheelbarrows. He looked at us.

"No. 1, Sissy," he said seriously, "I need those wheelbarrows."

"Take them, Papa," I said.

Sissy nodded.

Our father took the wheelbarrows. He loaded one into the other.

"You are good children," he said.

Without saying another word, without saying goodbye, Papa pushed the wheelbarrows down the road in the direction of the city. Grandfather and Sissy and I watched. Papa ran.

Two days later, the taxi man came with an envelope for Mama. In that envelope was money from Papa. Enough money for Grandmother to go to the medical center, and for a taxi too.

Mama shouted and cried. Mama Coca-Cola started to shout, "Taxi! Taxi!" even though the taxi man was already there.

Grandfather rose to his feet and started to praise God. Sissy started to cry. And all the aunties came to carry Grandmother gently and place her in the taxi next to Mama. We waved goodbye.

Grandfather and I watched the road for two days. On the third day Mama and Grandmother came back. Grandmother was on her own two feet. For the second time in one week Grandfather ran up the road. For the second time he was overtaken. But when at last he reached her, the person who held onto her the longest was Grandfather himself.

One month after that, the taxi man passed again. Again he stopped. This time he had a photograph for us.

A photograph of my father.

In the photograph Papa was standing with another man. They were both pushing wheelbarrows loaded high with sacks and bags and boxes.

"This is your father's new business," the taxi man explained. "He carries people's goods from one place to another. And this is his business partner."

We all looked closely at the photograph. On my father's face was a big smile.

I saw that on Sissy's face and Mama's face and Grandmother's face and Grandfather's face there was a big smile too. But not on mine.

Every time I heard a four-by-four I went down to the river to hide.

"What are you doing here?" asked Uncle Go-Easy. "Is that not your friend's four-by-four that I hear?"

I did not say anything.

"Do you not like choco-whatever anymore?" Uncle Go-Easy persisted.

I did not say anything.

"The man give you wheelbarrow to save Grandmother's life and you don' like him anymore?" Uncle Go-Easy was not giving up.

"He said wheelbarrow was to improve village life!" I said, trying not to cry.

"And so?" Uncle Go-Easy did not understand.

"I signed," I said, "to improve village life."

"Is that so?" said Uncle Go-Easy.

"And Papa took them to the city," I concluded, crying.

"Ahhh," Uncle Go-Easy nodded his head.

He took me
gently by the arm
and steered me
back towards the
village.

"Look!" he said,
nodding towards
our compound.

There were Beke
and Bisi and Bola and Sunshine and Smile
and all the other small babies playing with
Grandmother.

Uncle Go-Easy cocked his ear towards the
farms.

I could hear their mothers, the aunties,
along with my mother, singing as they hoed
their fields together without babies on their
backs or under their feet.

"We will eat well next year!" they sang.

"Look!" Uncle Go-Easy pointed back
down the path.

Sissy and her friend Nike were walking to the river with buckets of washing. Laughing!

"Look again!" He pointed up to the iroko tree.

Underneath the tree Grandfather was sitting happily, chanting the Odu Ifa and waving his fly swat. People sat beside him, drinking in his words and nodding their heads.

Suddenly I understood! The two
wheelbarrows in the city had made all
these people happy. They meant that
we would all eat well next year. In fact,
two wheelbarrows in the city were a big
improvement on village life!

I looked up at Uncle Go-Easy.

"Go easy, No. 1," he said, walking back to
the river.

I watched him go. Then I heard the
four-by-four engine even clearer. I looked up
at the road. I could not see it clearly yet but
I knew.

"Mike! Hi, Mike!" I shouted and ran
towards the road.

As I passed I heard
Grandfather shout,
"You see that
boy? He is the
No. 1! The No. 1
car spotter in the
world!"

Atinuke was born in Nigeria and spent her childhood in both Africa and the UK. She works as a storyteller in schools and in theatres, telling traditional African tales and reading from her books about Anna Hibiscus, and also the No.1 car spotter. *The No.1 Car Spotter* is her fifth book. Atinuke lives with her husband and two young sons in Wales.

Warwick Johnson Cadwell lives by the Sussex seaside with his smashing family and pets. Most of his time is spent drawing or thinking about drawing but for a change of scenery he also skippers boats.